Little Sisters Are...

Beth Norling

Kane/Miller
BOOK PUBLISHERS

Little sisters are

tiny...

cuddly...

smelly...

and sad.

Little sisters are

bitey...

spotty...

crunchy...

and loud.

Little sisters are

bouncy...

lumpy...

sticky...

and brave.

Little sisters are

floppy...

frowny...

and *fast.*

Little sisters can hide

in small places.

They make you laugh.

They are smart.

They are silly,

but best of all...

a little sister is your best friend.

I love my little sister.